ROOTS
PICTURE BOOKS

Title of original edition
Otto l'accessoiriste

Edited by
John McCarthy

Proofreading by
Ben Torrent

Typesetting by
Barbara Dusk

© Editions Langue au Chat, Liège, Belgium
© for this edition by Tom eMusic (New York 2016)

ISBN 978-1-62321-173-8

www.tomemusic.com
New York 2016

Otto
the Tinkerer

Vincent Zabus
Renaud Collin

Translated
by Adam Fisher

The old orphanage was a sombre and dreary place. Tim, who had never known his father, had to move here after his poor mother died. All he had left of her was an old photograph from when he was a baby, which he kept in his small treasure box with his favorite toys and a few candies. Ever since his mother died, Tim had not been able to say a single word. Not even a whisper. He quite simply, all of a sudden, stopped talking. Nobody could work out what was wrong with his voice. No matter how hard he tried to speak, scream or shout, not a single sound came out. The other children at the orphanage sometimes made fun of him because he couldn't talk, but Tim just ignored them. He spent his days sitting glumly on his bed, thinking about his mother and wondering about the world outside the orphanage. He often dreamt about sneaking out to explore the town, just as the other boys often did at night. Alas, unlike them, he simply did not dare.

me daddy

mom

One day, Tim heard two of the other little boys at the orphanage talking about a strange, old house on the other side of town, which they had seen the nights before. The stories they told about that old house were fantastic: at night you could see lights through the windows and hear the clanking of metal on metal all night long. The house's only resident was a big, rugged old man called Otto, who rarely left his curious house. "It's because of his job," people whispered. Rumor had it that he stayed up all night making things in there. What things? Nobody knew. Nobody ever went in. Of course, all of the boys at the orphanage had seen the old house, and they all had their own opinion about what old man Otto made in there; all of them except Tim, that is. Tim was still afraid to leave the orphanage, and when the other boys asked him if he wanted to go and see the old house, Tim simply shook his head.

The other boys, of course, teased Tim, calling him a complete scaredy-cat.

After a time, Tim grew tired of hearing from the other boys what a wimp he was and decided to prove how brave he could be. One fateful night, he resolved that not only would he go to see Otto's workshop, but he'd also go where no one else had gone before...

Soon after, Tim found himself standing on the doorstep to Otto's workshop. He slowly pushed the front door open and tiptoed inside. His eyes were immediately met by an incredible sight. The room was huge and filled with strange and wondrous objects scattered around the room and stacked on shelves that almost reached the ceiling: witches' brooms, a wizard's hat, pirate hooks, a sword, a glass slipper, magic wands, poison apples and a many more amazing things.

Just as the boy was about to pick up one of the magic wands, he heard the front door begin to creak open, and he jumped behind a large plant pot.

Not a second later, a white rabbit hopped through the front door and called out: "Mr Otto! Mr Otto! Is my clock ready yet? I need it rather urgently; Alice is worried, you see..."

Tim peeped out from behind his hiding place, hoping to get a look at the mysterious old man. First Tim heard a deep sigh from the next room, and then he saw Otto himself: a tall, broad-shouldered old man, who walked into the room, holding an old clock and muttering grumpily under his breath.

Tim peeked even further out to get a better look at the old man, but as he did so, the pumpkin he had been leaning against tumbled off the plant pot and bumped loudly on the floor. As soon as it did, it transformed itself into a giant horse-drawn carriage…

"What the devil?!" exclaimed Otto, seeing the boy now hanging from the pumpkin carriage by the collar of his tee shirt. "Who the 'ell let you in 'ere?! Ya sneaky little urchin!"

Tim did not answer...or rather could not.

Otto growled again in his face:

"What's your name, boy?!"

Tim looked at Otto with a terrified look in his eyes.

"Unbelievable! Am I going deaf or have I actually found a kid that doesn't talk?! Hmmm, well I never…" muttered Otto, freeing the boy from his uncomfortable perch. The look of terror in Tim's eyes was slowly replaced by curiosity. The old man showed the boy to a seat in the corner of his workshop and headed over to a workbench where he continued his work on a half-woven basket. Tim sat and watched the old Tinkerer for an hour, neither one of them uttering a word to the other.

"This is for Little Red Riding Hood," Otto broke the silence at last, "and I'm a Tinkerer—I make and repair magical objects for my clients who come from the Land of Fairy Tales. Without me, half the fairy tales told to kids like you wouldn't exist! And I can tell you one thing: it isn't an easy job, making these miracles!"

From then on Tim began to visit the old man every day; Tim loved watching him work, as it helped him forget his woes. The old man also seemed to enjoy Tim's silent company.

Today was Tim's birthday. Tim always missed his mother the most on his birthday. Sitting in his cold, hard bed, Tim thought that he would be much happier living with Otto and helping him with his work. Suddenly he had a great idea—*why not ask Otto if he could come and live with him?*
Tim decided to drop the question that very night. But how could he ask if he couldn't speak?
Sure enough, once in Otto's workshop, Tim tried to ask the question several times as hard as he could, but as always, he remained hopelessly silent. The Tinkerer, upon seeing the boy try so desperately to speak, stroked his head and comforted him: "Don't worry, boy, you'll tell me some other time."

Just as the boy heaved a sigh of disappointment,
all of a sudden a bird came crashing with a thud into
the workshop. Tim noticed that the bird was carrying a note,
which Otto gently plucked from its beak. The Tinkerer
hastily opened the letter and began to read it aloud:
"One of the seven-league boots has been torn…"
Otto broke off, his face white as a sheet.
"Sorry, Tim, I have to leave.
Duty calls!" he shouted
as he pulled on his coat
and disappeared behind
a door.

Tim, now left alone, started to think frantically: *I wonder...if I were to help Otto on his new mission...perhaps he'd make me his apprentice and let me stay with him? Well, it's worth a try!*

Determined to prove his worth to the Tinkerer, Tim boldly followed the old man through the door and up the wooden staircase where Tim was blasted by a strong wind that grew stronger with each step. At the top of the stairs the boy found a large, round, open window and beyond it, an unusual sight…

O tto was standing on a platform. In front of him was a large mechanical bird perched on a long pole. The bird was Otto's own design, cobbled together from scrap metal from many of the magical objects he tinkered with.

As Otto prepared
the bird for flight,
Tim saw his chance—he
clambered up the next flight
of stairs and stowed away
in a large leather bag.
Otto, unaware of the extra
cargo, attached the bag under
the bird's wing.

"Squaaawk! Welcome aboard! Welcome aboard!" shrieked the bird in its metallic voice. "Squaaawk! Lot's to do tonight, Otto: one of the seven-league boots has been torn in two! Where to, sir?! Squaaawk!"
The seven-league boots were a magical pair of boots that allowed the wearer to travel seven leagues in a single step! To repair them, Otto would need some very rare materials that could only be found in three places throughout the Land of Fairy Tales.

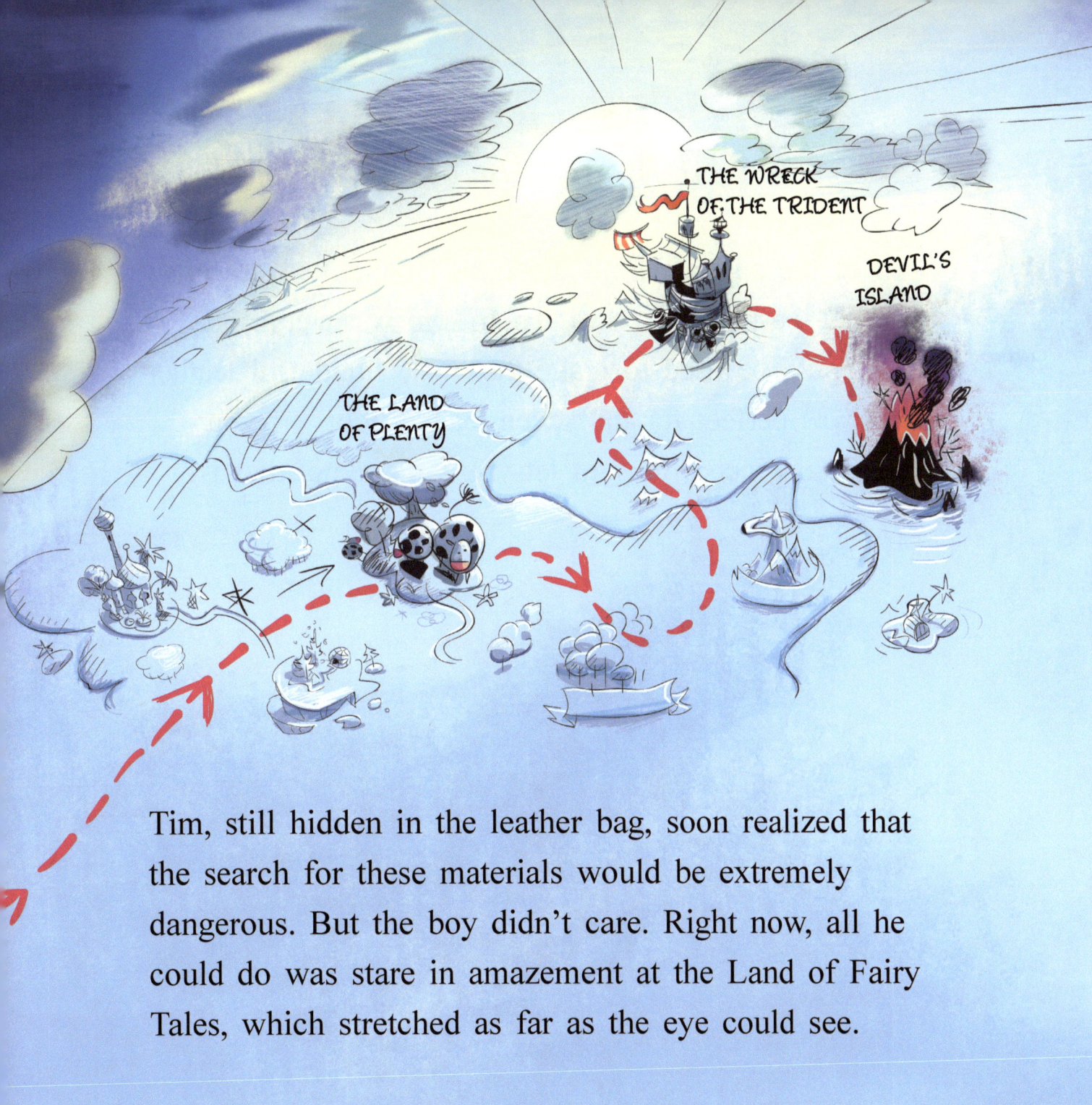

Tim, still hidden in the leather bag, soon realized that the search for these materials would be extremely dangerous. But the boy didn't care. Right now, all he could do was stare in amazement at the Land of Fairy Tales, which stretched as far as the eye could see.

The First Quest:
THE LAND OF PLENTY

All of the animals from the Land of Plenty were big and fat—especially cows. Their skin was very soft and could be used to make the most wonderful leather that was perfect for the seven-league boots, if you could convince a cow to let you take some, that is!

The Tinkerer knew just what to do! He found the oldest, wrinkliest cow in the field and offered to make her look young again. First he stretched and smoothed out the skin so that it looked pretty and wrinkle-free, and then he removed the extra bits.

Tim watched undetected as the Tinkerer went about his work, that is until the old man folded up the cow's skin and tried to put it in his bag!

"Ow!" shouted Tim as his head was almost squashed.

"What the devil are you doing in there?" yelled Otto.

"Who told you that you could come with me?" He grabbed the boy by the collar and lifted him angrily. "I ought to send you right back to the orphanage!"

"Sqwaaawk! No time for that! We still have to…" shrieked the bird, before it was rudely interrupted.

"…I know what we have to do, you silly, old piece of junk!" snarled the Tinkerer as he gave the bird a heavy whack to the head. Despite having been thumped over the head, the bird repeated itself: "No time for that! We still have to find the other items to repair the boots. Squaaawk!"

Otto let out a long groan and put Tim on the bird's back.

WHACK

The Second Quest:
THE WRECK OF THE TRIDENT

"Now we have to find the wreck of the Trident," the bird screeched.

Legend had it that one day, a giant whale found an old trade ship called the Trident, which had been shipwrecked against some incredibly sharp and dangerous rocks, spilling out enormous rolls of cotton thread into the ocean.

The whale had bad breath, but no way to clean its huge teeth, and so it took the rolls of cotton thread in its mouth and tied them around the rocks, so that after every meal, it could bite down on the threads and use them to clean between its teeth. Now Otto, of course, knew that this thread was incredibly strong and perfect for repairing the seven-league boots!

"The problem is," said Otto, "that the whale refuses to share the thread with anyone.
So we might struggle to get some."

"Dental floss on the starboard side!" screeched the bird after a long hour of searching the ocean. Otto took out a pair of special scissors and got ready to cut the thread, when suddenly the whale's huge tail came rushing up from beneath the waves, only to crash back down on the water's surface, sending water flying into the air!

The terrible whale swam towards them at a fantastic speed, ready to swallow them whole! The mechanical bird turned sharply to avoid the whale's perfectly clean and terrifying teeth, but then suddenly dropped out of the sky, heading straight for the water. Otto realized that the bird had switched off—he must have damaged it when he hit it over the head! Otto did what he normally did when the bird stopped working and bashed it in the head a second time. The bird started up again, but it was too late!

All three of them crashed with
a loud bang into one of the rocks.
As Otto regained his senses, he turned
to make sure Tim was not hurt,
but the boy was nowhere to be found.
"Where on Earth could he be?"
the old man shouted in a wild frenzy.

But Tim was safe and sound. Before they crashed into the rock, the boy had leaped from the bird's back and grabbed one of the huge cotton threads.

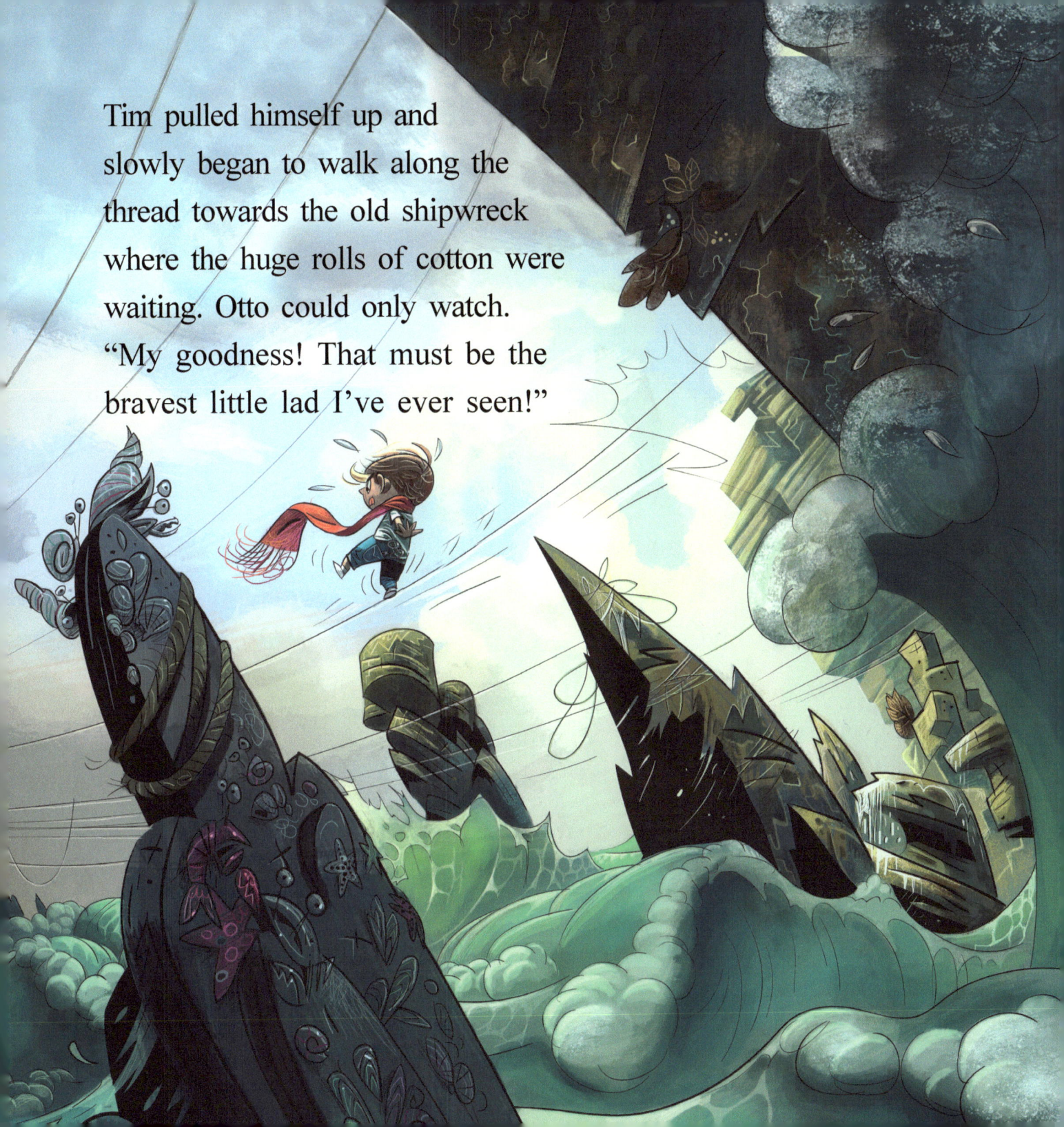

Tim pulled himself up and slowly began to walk along the thread towards the old shipwreck where the huge rolls of cotton were waiting. Otto could only watch. "My goodness! That must be the bravest little lad I've ever seen!"

Tim somehow made it across the thread to the old shipwreck and managed to cut off enough thread.

"Squaaawk! Nice job!" crowed the bird as it gently caught Tim in its claws.

"Well done, lad!" shouted Otto over the roar of the waves. If Tim could speak, he would have asked the Tinkerer to accept him as his apprentice. *Otto would definitely agree now,* thought Tim. But the boy did not even try to ask. He knew that he wouldn't be able to produce so much as a whisper. Now the three adventurers would face the third and most dangerous quest. They had to go to Devil's Island where Otto had to find some nails from the Devil's workshop. These were virtually indestructible, and only these nails could be used to fasten the soles of the seven-league boots!

The Third Quest:
DEVIL'S ISLAND

"Tim, you stay here, at the foot of the volcano," said
the Tinkerer. "It's not safe here for a young kid like you.
It's better if I go alone this time!"

Otto was so worried about the boy that he didn't even
notice the huge, black shadow standing over him…

Tim's eyes widened and his mouth dropped open as
he looked up into the Devil's face. He had to warn Otto!
He tried to scream 'Look out!' but alas not a single
sound came out of his gaping mouth.

"What's the matter with you?" asked Otto, just before
he received a heavy blow to the back of his head…

Surprised but not defeated, Otto attempted to fight
back against the horrific beast.

The Tinkerer's mechanical companion tried to help him, but the Devil knocked the creature unconscious with a single blow. The Devil began to strangle Otto.

The old man fought as hard as he could, but he was almost out of breath! The Tinkerer was doomed! Doomed because of Tim, who hadn't been able to utter even two simple words… Tim felt his anger growing inside him. He thought of his father who had abandoned him, saw the sad eyes of his dying mother, heard the taunts and insults from the other children at the orphanage. And now his only true friend was going to die because of him!

Tim's anger bubbled and grew until it became unbearable, and finally turned into a powerful, ear-splitting scream: "ARRRGGGHHH!!"

The Devil suddenly released Otto. Looking at Tim in complete confusion, he clapped his hands over his ears. How could someone so small produce such an earth-shattering cry?

Otto saw his chance at once and dealt the Devil a mighty blow. The dark figure hissed and stumbled backward before falling with a huge thud to the ground… The Devil had been defeated! The Tinkerer took the nails from the monster's cloak before turning to Tim.

"Listen, I don't know how to put it… But you see, I'm growing old… I've been thinking of finding someone who could help me with my work and… I think you'd make a perfect apprentice!"

Tim looked intently into the old man's eyes,
slowly opened his mouth…

A nd he began to speak…

The Tinkerer's mechanical bird gave a happy squawk, and the old man's eyes filled with tears of joy! On the way back to Otto's workshop, Tim finally felt free—free to speak, shout and even sing along with Otto:

Who can turn a pumpkin into a carriage?—the Tinkerer can!
Who can make a rabbit's clock out of a cabbage?—the
Tinkerer can!
Who can mend the seven-league boots?
Who can build an owl that hoots?
Otto the Tinkerer man!

www.ingramcontent.com/pod-product-compliance
Lightning Source LLC
Chambersburg PA
CBHW041001170626
46815CB00002B/107